WHAT PET TO GET?

Spencer

For Conrad and Imogen, with all my love
—Emma xx

If you'd like to learn more about adopting a pet, please contact your local chapter of the
American Society for the Prevention of Cruelty to Animals, or go to www.aspca.org.

Text and illustrations © 2006 by Emma Dodd

All rights reserved. Published by Arthur A. Levine Books, an imprint of Scholastic Inc.,
Publishers since 1920, by arrangement with Templar Publishing, an imprint of
The Templar Company plc, The Granary, North Street, Surrey, RH4 1DN, England. SCHOLASTIC and
the LANTERN LOGO are trademarks and/or registered trademarks of Scholastic Inc.

Library of Congress Cataloging-in-Publication Data
Dodd, Emma, 1969–
What pet to get? / Emma Dodd. — 1st American ed.
p. cm.
Summary: Jack's mother agrees that he may have a pet, but when he suggests everything
from an elephant to a tyrannosaurus rex, she must explain why each would be less than ideal.
ISBN 0-545-03570-8 [1. Pets—Fiction. 2. Mothers and sons—Fiction.] I. Title.
PZ7.D6626Wha 2008
[E] —dc22
2007010106
ISBN-13: 978-0-545-04466-0
ISBN-10: 0-545-04466-9

10 9 8 7 6 5 4 3 2 1   08 09 10 11 12

First Scholastic paperback printing, January 2008
Printed in the U.S.A.   03

WHAT PET TO GET?

Emma Dodd

Arthur A. Levine Books   An Imprint of Scholastic Inc.

"Let's get a pet," said Jack one day.
"I **promise** I'll look after it."

"If you like, dear," replied his mother
absentmindedly.
"**What** pet should we get?"

Jack thought about it for a little while.
"I think we should get an elephant," he announced.
"I could **ride** it to school."

SCHOOL

"An elephant would be nice, dear," said Mom,
"but not very practical.
How would we take it on vacation?"

"On the roof rack, of course," said Jack.

"I don't think so, dear," said Mom.
"It might squash the car."

"Hmm, maybe **not** an elephant then,"
said Jack.

"What about a lion?" he said.
"I'd remember to **feed**
it **every** day."

"That would be super, dear,"
replied Mom,
"but lions do have very
big appetites . . .

. . . and anyway, it would frighten the mail carrier."

"Hmm, I hadn't thought of **that**," said Jack.

Jack thought some more.

"I think we should get a polar bear," he said.
"It would make a **great** playmate."

"A polar bear would be lovely, dear," replied his mother.
"But I don't think it would like the central heating."

"Hmm, I **suppose** not," agreed Jack.

Jack thought some more.
What pet to get?

"Could we get a *Tyrannosaurus rex*?"
he asked.

"I could take it for **walks**."

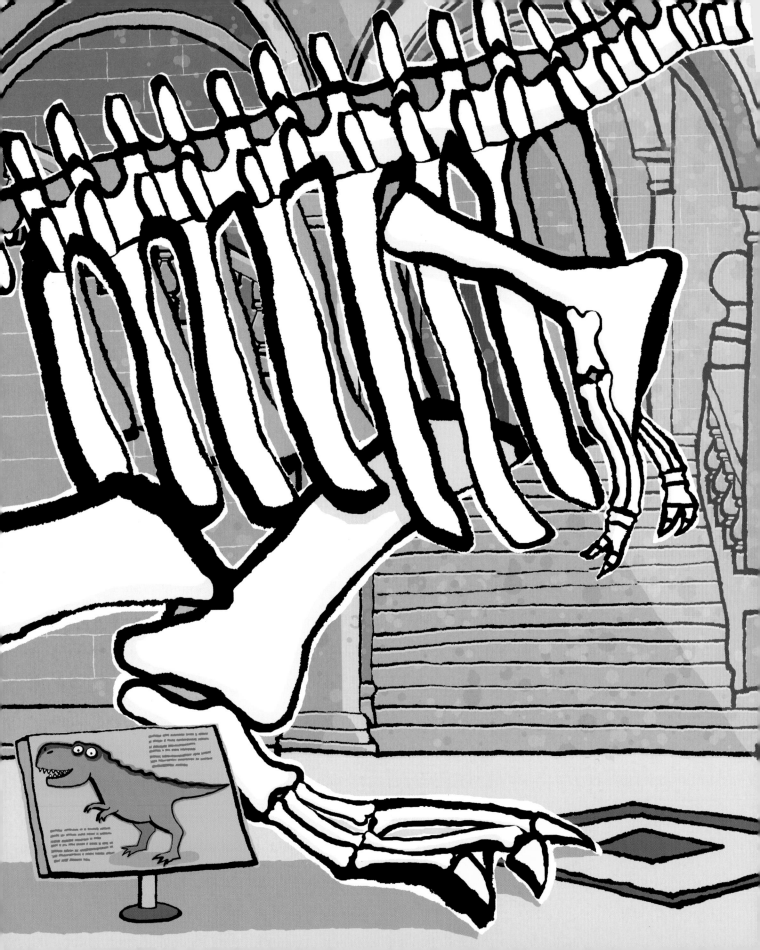

"That **would** have been a great idea, dear," replied Mom, "but unfortunately the *Tyrannosaurus rex* has been **extinct** for sixty-five million years."

"What a shame," said Jack. "Well, what about . . .

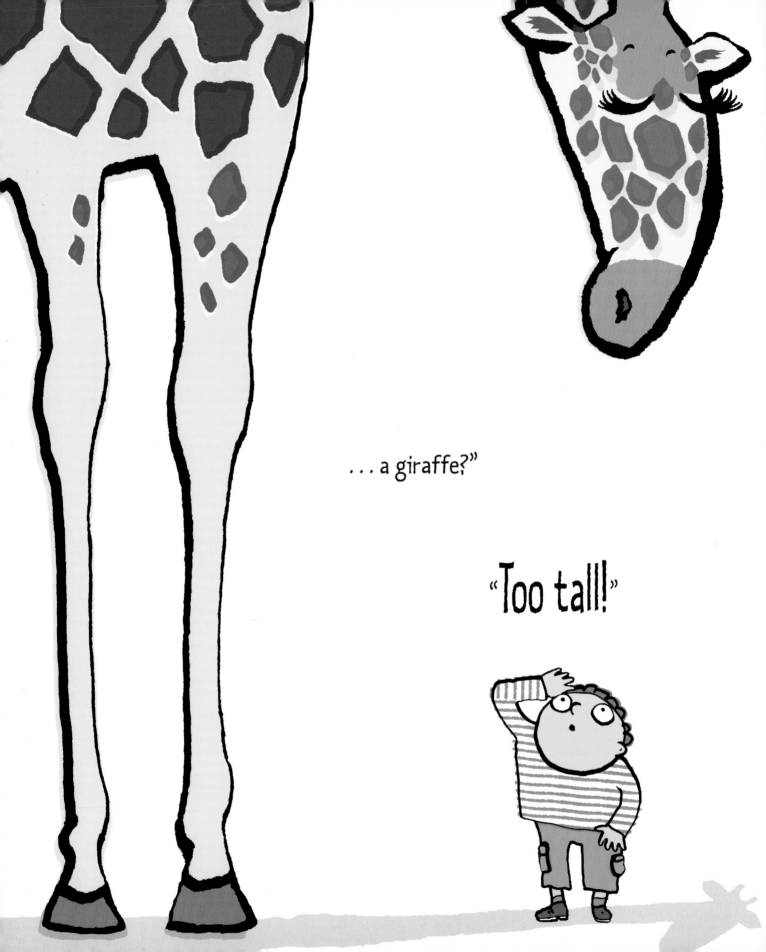

". . . a giraffe?"

"Too tall!"

"I suppose a **shark** is out of the question?"

"Yes, dear," sighed Mom.
"Perhaps you could try to think of something less . . .
exotic."

Early the next morning, Jack announced,

"I've got it!
Let's get a dog!"

"That's an **excellent** idea, dear,"
said Mom.
"We'll go this morning and choose . . .

...a lovely **little** puppy!"